CLASSIC FAIRY TALES

Brown Watson

England

© 1989 Brown Watson (Leicester) Ltd.

CONTENTS

RED RIDING HOOD

One morning Little Red Riding
Hood's mother asked her to take a
basket of food to her Grandma who
was in bed and not feeling very
well. "Do go straight to Grandma's
house," said her mother and
dressed her in her red cape and
hood.

4

On her way through the wood, Little Red Riding Hood met a wolf who asked her where she was going. "To see my Grandma who is ill in bed," said Little Red Riding Hood.

"Where does she live?" asked the wolf. "At the cottage in the wood," said Little Red Riding Hood without thinking, and before she knew what had happened the wolf turned and ran off.

5

The wolf rushed straight to the cottage where Grandma lived and when he arrived he knocked at the door. "Who is there?" called Grandma, and the wolf replied, "It's Little Red Riding Hood, Grandma." "Lift the latch and come in," said Grandma. When she saw the wolf she was so frightened, she hid herself in the cupboard.

The wolf quickly put on Grandma's bed-cap and waited for Little Red Riding Hood to arrive. "Who is there?" he called in a voice like Grandma's when he heard her knock. "It is Little Red Riding Hood," she answered. "Lift the latch and come in," said the wolf.

"How are you feeling?" said Little Red Riding Hood. "Much better thank you dear," said the wolf and as he spoke, his bed cap slipped from his head so that Little Red Riding Hood could see his ears. "What big ears you have!" said Little Red Riding Hood nervously. "All the better to hear you with," said the wolf.

"What big teeth you have," cried Little Red Riding Hood. "All the better to eat you with," shouted the wolf as he jumped out of the bed. "You are not my Grandma!" screamed Little Red Riding Hood. "No, I am the big bad wolf, and I am going to eat you up!"

As Little Red Riding Hood ran from the house, a woodcutter who was cutting some trees outside heard her cries for help. He chased the wolf down the path and the wolf ran off into the woods as fast as he could.

The woodcutter took Little Red Riding Hood back into the cottage to see if the nasty wolf had eaten her Grandma. As they called her, a voice said, "I am in the cupboard, is it safe to come out?" When Grandma heard Little Red Riding Hood's voice she knew that all was well.

"How lucky we both are to be safe!" said Little Red Riding Hood as she hugged her Grandma.

They both thanked the woodcutter and asked him to stay for tea.

CINDERELLA

Cinderella lived in a big house with her father and two stepsisters. The stepsisters were very unkind to her and made her do all the housework. Although she was pretty they made her dress in rags instead of nice clothes.

Cinderella's stepsisters spent most of their time in front of the mirror powdering their noses and making Cinderella brush their hair.

12

One day an invitation to the ball
arrived from the palace.
"May I go?" asked Cinderella.

Cinderella's stepsisters
laughed and said that it was
impossible. This made
Cinderella very sad. When
her stepsisters finally left for
the ball, Cinderella sat
crying by the fire.

Cinderella was quite alone in the house, and was surprised to hear a voice saying, "I am your Fairy Godmother, and you shall go to the ball. Bring me a pumpkin, four white mice and three lizards."

As fast as lightning, the pumpkin was changed into a coach, the four white mice into four lovely white horses and the lizards into a coach driver and two footmen.

When the Fairy Godmother waved her wand, Cinderella's rags changed into a wonderful ball dress and she had dainty glass slippers on her feet. "You must leave the palace before twelve o' clock, or everything will change back to how it was before," her Fairy Godmother told her.

Cinderella so enjoyed dancing with the Prince that she forgot the time and soon the clock struck twelve. She ran quickly down the palace steps. As she ran, the Prince tried to stop her, but she was gone.

The Prince found one of Cinderella's tiny glass slippers and told his footmen, "I will marry the girl whose foot it will fit!"

The footmen travelled for many miles in search of the owner, and, on their way back to the palace, they called at Cinderella's house. The two stepsisters tried to make the slipper fit them, but it was no use.

Just as they were leaving, Cinderella's father said that she should be allowed to try the slipper. It fitted her perfectly. Cinderella married the Prince and became the happiest girl in the land.

SLEEPING BEAUTY

Many years ago a King and Queen told everyone of the birth of their baby. The fairies in the land brought the baby gifts, but one wicked fairy promised that when the Princess was fifteen years old, she would prick her finger and go to sleep for one hundred years.

On her fifteenth birthday, the Princess took a walk through her castle and found a room where an old woman sat spinning. "Will you show me how to spin?" the Princess asked.

The old woman showed her what to do but when she touched the needle she pricked her finger and fell asleep at once, and so did everyone else in the castle.

Years passed and one day a handsome Prince was riding by the castle and decided to take a look inside. He was surprised to find that everyone was asleep.

Soon he found the Princess and thought how beautiful she was. He knelt down by her side and kissed her.

At that moment the spell was broken and the Princess and all the other people in the castle woke up from their deep sleep.

The Princess told the Prince the story of the wicked fairy's spell and how she had pricked her finger.

Soon the Prince and the Princess fell in love with each other and decided to marry.

The King and Queen arranged a lovely wedding for their daughter and her Prince and all the townsfolk and servants in the castle danced and danced until the next morning.

The Prince and Princess and everyone in the castle lived happily ever after.

SNOW WHITE

and the seven dwarfs

Once upon a time there was a little princess whose skin was so fair that they called her Snow White. She had a stepmother who every day asked her mirror, "Mirror, mirror on the wall, who is the fairest of them all?"

The mirror had always told the Queen that she was the fairest, until one day it said that Snow White was fairer. The Queen was so angry that she told a servant to take Snow White to the woods and kill her.

The servant could not bring himself to kill Snow White but set her free to wander in the woods. Soon she found a tiny cottage where seven little dwarfs lived.

When they arrived home from their work that day, Snow White asked them if she could stay with them and they agreed.

The next day the Queen asked the mirror the usual question but to her horror the mirror replied, "Queen, thou art beauty rare, but Snow White living in the glen with seven little men is many times more beautiful!"

The Queen was very angry and, dressed as an old woman, she went and tried to sell Snow White a petticoat ribbon which would have squeezed her to death, but Snow White refused.

Later that day the Queen visited the cottage again and gave Snow White a rosy apple. Snow White took one bite and fell to the ground poisoned.

One day a Prince arrived in the forest and took Snow White from the glass case in which she lay. The piece of poisoned apple fell from her throat and she awoke. The Queen died shortly after and Snow White and the Prince lived happily ever after.